The Moogees Move House

Leslie McGuirk

CANDLEWICK PRESS

THERE ONCE WAS a mama Moogee,
a papa Moogee, and three little Moogees.
They lived in a house built on very tall stilts . . .
with way too many stairs.

Mama Moogee said,
"We need a new place that is on the ground.
It would be nice if it was round."

Papa Moogee said,
"I'd like to find a home with class
and a nice wide yard and plenty of grass."

The three little Moogees all screamed,

"Waa Waa moogee doogee

Wee wee low lum!"

They began their search by driving to the real-estate office.
A Moogee came out and introduced himself as Mr. Ruru.

"What a happy family you seem to be!
I have lots of houses for you to see."

The Moogees and Mr. Ruru piled into the Moogeemobile and drove to the first house, a great big blue house with large windows, eight chimneys, and a yukie-yukie tree loaded with yukie-yukie berries.

THAT PLACE OVER THERE iS FOR SALE!

Mama Moogee said,
"Of course, this house will never do.
I'm not particularly fond of blue."

Papa Moogee took one look at the price and said,
"You'd have to be a millionaire
to afford a house like that one there."

The three little Moogees all screamed,

'waa waa moogee doogee

wee wee low lum!"

So they ventured onward and arrived at a home
with large statues lining the driveway.

Mr. Ruru said,
"This charming place is up for sale.
It even comes with a pet snail."

Mama Moogee looked at Mr. Ruru and said,
"The yard and snail are quite delightful,
but those statues are truly frightful."

Papa Moogee looked at Mama Moogee and said,
"I agree.
Let's move on to house number three."

The three little Moogees all screamed,

'waa Waa moogee doogee

Wee wee low lum!"

Mr. Ruru was sure they would love the next house.
It looked exactly like a hunk of cheese, and Mr. Ruru
adored cheese.

Mr. Ruru said,

"This house here is quite a steal.
Maybe we could make a deal!"

Mama Moogee looked at the house and shook her head. "Mr. Ruru, I am afraid this house would only be perfect for a mouse."

Papa Moogee sniffed the house and said, "I don't want to sound unkind, but a stinky cheese house is not what we had in mind."

The three little Moogees all screamed,

'waa Waa moogee doogee

Wee wee low lum!"

Mr. Ruru had only one house left. He worried that it was all wrong, too. As they drove toward it, Mr. Ruru wondered if the Moogee family would like it.

As they pulled into the driveway, he said,
"Even though this house is pink,
I'd still like to know what you think!"

Mama Moogee said,
"Finally a house that's round,
and it's even on the ground."

Papa Moogee said,
"This house is what we've been looking for!
It's got a nice big lawn and a handsome door!"

Mr. Ruru smiled as the Moogees discussed how nicely the roof was tiled.

Mr. Ruru said, "You can even move in today!"
He looked at Mama Moogee.

She said, "OK!"
And Papa Moogee said, "Hooray!"

Which made all those little Moogees jump and play.

And then of course, they proceeded to say . . .

"waa waa

wee wee

moogee doogee

low lum!"

And that's when Mr. Ruru finally understood what those little Moogees had been saying all along:

"We'll be happy anywhere as long as we've got our family there!"

For Bert
A Moogee in spirit

First edition 2012

Library of Congress Cataloging-in-Publication Data is available.

Library of Congress Catalog Card Number pending

ISBN 978-0-7636-5558-7

12 13 14 15 16 17 SCP 10 9 8 7 6 5 4 3 2 1

Printed in Humen, Dongguan, China

This book was typeset in Agenda and hand-lettered by the author.
The illustrations were done in marker.

Candlewick Press
99 Dover Street
Somerville, Massachusetts 02144

visit us at www.candlewick.com